ELLa MaY AND THE WiSHiNG STONe

Illustrated by
CARY FAGAN   GENEVIÈVE CÔTÉ

TUNDRA BOOKS

Published in Canada by Tundra Books, a division of Random House of Canada Limited,
One Toronto Street, Suite 300, Toronto, Ontario M5C 2V6

Published in the United States by Tundra Books of Northern New York,
P.O. Box 1030, Plattsburgh, New York 12901

Library of Congress Control Number: 2010938591

Library and Archives Canada Cataloguing in Publication

Fagan, Cary
    Ella May and the wishing stone / Cary Fagan ; illustrated by Geneviève Côté.

ISBN 978-1-77049-225-7

    I. Côté, Geneviève, 1964- II. Title.

PS8561.A375E55 2011   jC813'.54   C2010-906382-1

We acknowledge the financial support of the Government of Canada through the Book Publish-
ing Industry Development Program (BPIDP) and that of the Government of Ontario through the
Ontario Media Development Corporation's Ontario Book Initiative.
We further acknowledge the support of the Canada Council for the Arts and the Ontario Arts
Council for our publishing program.

ONTARIO ARTS COUNCIL
CONSEIL DES ARTS DE L'ONTARIO

Medium: digital

Design: Leah Springate

Printed and bound in China

  2 3 4 5 6   16 15 14 13 12

For Hélène Comay

– C.F.

*For my friends, who so willingly and generously
share their own wishing stones*

– G.C.

When Ella May came home from the beach, she sat on the step of her porch. She still wore her bathing suit, sunglasses, hat, and flip-flops. She held a smooth stone in her hand and, while she sat, she sang a little song.

"Wish, wish, I'm making a wish
On my wishing stone.
And it will come true, oh yes it will,
Because I brought you home."

Ella May's best friend, Manuel, lived next door.
When he heard her singing, Manuel ran right over.

"You're back!" Manuel said. "Want to play
hopscotch?"

"No, thanks," Ella May said. "Look what I
have." She held out her hand and opened her
fingers.

"It's a stone," Manuel said.

"It isn't just a stone. It's a wishing stone. See?
It has a line going all-all-all the way around it.
That's what makes it a wishing stone. Now all my
wishes will come true."

"No, they won't," Manuel said.

"Yes, they will."

"Go ahead, then," Manuel said. "Wish
for something."

Ella May thought a moment. "I wish that I could show my special wishing stone to all my friends."

"That isn't much of a wish," Manuel said.

Her other friends on the block noticed that Ella May had come home. They came up to see her. Amir came. Maya came.

"Look," Ella May said. "I have a wishing stone." She held it out for them to see.

"Can I hold it?" Amir asked.

"Can I hold it, too?" Maya asked.

"Oh, no." Ella May put the stone in her lap. "It's too special."

Manuel watched the other kids. "I'm going to find my own wishing stone," he said.

They all started looking for their own wishing stones. They looked in the front gardens. They looked in the back gardens. They looked under trees and behind garbage cans.

Amir found a small flat stone.
Maya found a big round stone.
Manuel found a funny long stone.
They ran to show Ella May.

Ella May peered at Manuel's stone, tipping up her sunglasses so that she could see better. "Nope," she said happily.

She looked at Maya's stone, then at Amir's stone. "Nope and double nope," she said. "None of your stones has a line going all-all-all the way around it." She sang her little song.

*"Wish, wish, I'm making a wish
On my wishing stone.
And it will come true, oh yes it will,
Because I brought you home."*

The screen door of Ella May's house opened. Out slid a little tray. On the tray were a tuna fish sandwich, a pickle, a handful of chips, and a glass of milk.

"Look!" she said. "I wished for my lunch and here it is. Thank you, wishing stone."

"You're not nice," Manuel said. He put his stone in his pocket and tromped down the sidewalk to his own house.

Ella May watched him go. "Hey," she said. "I wanted Manuel to go home and he did. Thank you again, wishing stone."

But Manuel did not stay away for long. He came around from his back garden, pulling a wagon. On top of the wagon was a big cardboard box. There were all kinds of switches and buttons on the box. Written across the side were the words The Wishing Stone Company.

Manuel pulled the wagon right up in front of Ella May's house. In a loud voice, he called out: "Turn your ordinary stone into a wishing stone! Try our amazing new machine! Only one penny!"

Ella May came down off her porch to look at the box. "You can't turn an ordinary stone into a wishing stone," she said.

"Just wait and see," Manuel said. "Who wants a try?"

"I do!" Maya said. She fished in her pocket and came up with a sticky penny.

Manuel put the penny in his own pocket. "Just drop your stone in here," he said, pointing to a hole near the top of the box.

Maya pushed in her stone. A whirring sound started, and then a noise like air coming out of a balloon. The box began to shake. A bell rang, and the stone fell out the other end.

Maya picked up her stone. "*Ooh!*" everyone gasped. For sure enough, there was a line that went all-all-all the way around the stone.

"Do mine next!" Amir said.

Manuel's machine turned each stone into a wishing stone. The kids ran up and down the block, shouting out their wishes.

"I want a pony!" cried Maya.

"I want to walk on the moon!" sang Amir.

From her porch, Ella May watched as they ran about. She didn't think they wanted her to join them. And she didn't want to anyway.

"I wish I was the only one to have a wishing stone," she said.

It started to rain – a soft, warm summer rain that felt good on the skin. The kids danced around and around while Ella May watched from the porch.

But something started to happen. The lines on their wishing stones got blurry. Then they began to wash away.

Amir looked at his stone. It had become ordinary again. "Now my wish won't come true," he said. "I want my penny back."

"I do too!" said Maya.

Once again, Ella May was the only one with a wishing stone, but she didn't feel as happy as she thought she would.

Ella May tried to cheer herself up by singing her little song.

"*Wish, wish, I'm making a wish…*"

But it didn't work. She closed her eyes. "I wish I could have my friends back," she said. "I wish I didn't even have this old wishing stone."

And then she went into her house.

After a while she came out again, with her arms holding
a wooden crate full of things.

"What are you doing?" asked Manuel.

"You'll see," said Ella May. She took the wooden
crate and attached a broom handle to it, with the brush
part sticking up, and a ribbon at the back. Then she put
an old scrap of rug across the crate for a saddle.

"Here you go," she said, giving it to Maya.

"A pony!" Maya said. She got on, cried *yippee!* and
pretended to gallop across the prairie.

Ella May put egg cartons down on the sidewalk.

"What's that?" asked Amir.

"That's the surface of the moon," said Ella May. "But there's no air on the moon. You'll need this."

She made him a helmet from a cardboard box, tinfoil, and pipe cleaners for antennae.

Amir walked slowly over the egg cartons. "This is Astronaut Amir calling," he said. "I am now walking over the lunar surface. Over and out."

Ella May said to Manuel, "You never made a wish. What do you wish for?"

Manuel thought a minute. "I still want to play hopscotch."

So Ella May drew a hopscotch board on the sidewalk with a piece of chalk. The other kids used their ordinary stones as markers. But Ella May couldn't find her wishing stone.

They all helped her look for it. They looked on the porch, in the front gardens, in the back gardens, but they couldn't find it.

"Maybe wishing stones don't stay very long," Manuel said.

They found her an ordinary stone.

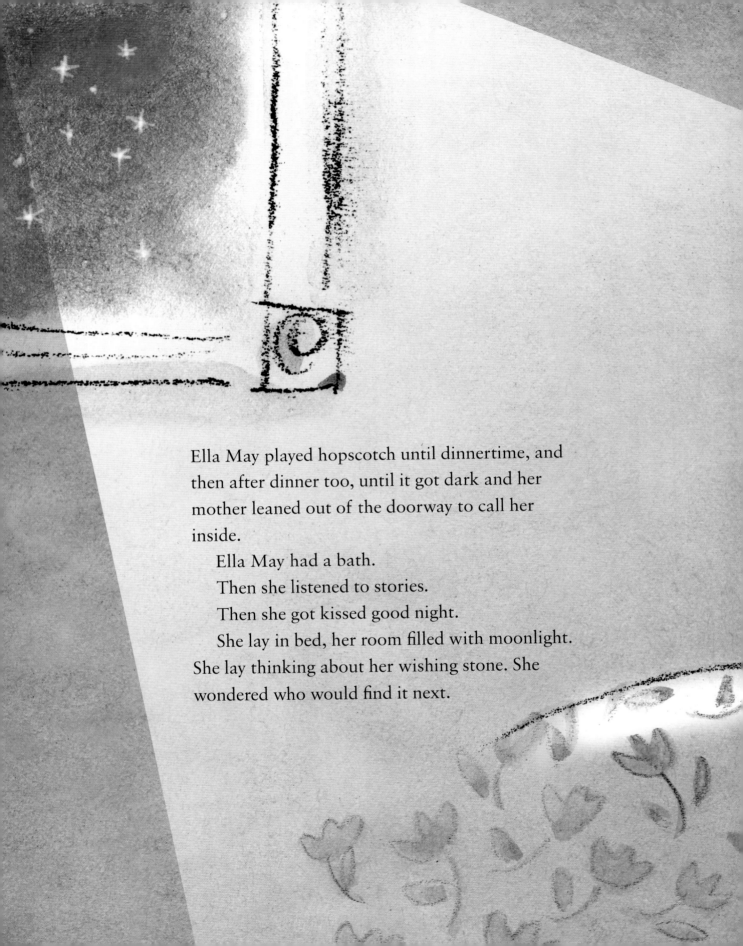

Ella May played hopscotch until dinnertime, and
then after dinner too, until it got dark and her
mother leaned out of the doorway to call her
inside.

    Ella May had a bath.

    Then she listened to stories.

    Then she got kissed good night.

    She lay in bed, her room filled with moonlight.
She lay thinking about her wishing stone. She
wondered who would find it next.

Ella May closed her eyes. "Thank you, wishing stone," she whispered.